Magic beans

"Look what I got for Skimmed Milk!" said Jack.
Dotty went nutty and threw the beans out of the window.

The next morning, Jack looked out of the window and saw a giant beanstalk growing out of the garden and into the sky.

Jack climbed the beanstalk to see where it led.

At the top was a huge castle.
Inside the castle, there was a tall table and chair.
"Someone big lives here," said Jack.

Then he saw a box filled with gold!
Jack grabbed the gold and put it in his pockets.

Suddenly, the door burst open
and a gigantic giant marched inside.

He roared:
"Fee fi fo fum, I smell the
blood of an Englishman.
Be he alive or be he dead,
I'll grind his bones
into my bread."

Fee fi fo fum!

The giant spotted Jack in the box of gold.
Jack jumped out and ran back to the beanstalk.

The giant followed Jack and roared:
"Fee fi fo fum, I smell the blood of an Englishman!
I'll have him steamed, I'll have him stewed,
I'll have him boiled or barbecued!"

Jack reached the bottom of the beanstalk
and shouted to his mother, "Get an axe!"

Chop!

Chop!

Chop!

Jack chopped and chopped until
there was a creak and a crack and . . .
the beanstalk fell down!
The giant fell to the ground too,
and that was the end of him.

Jack showed his mother the gold.
"We've hit the jackpot, Jack Pott!" she said with a grin.

Jack bought Skimmed Milk back,
and they all lived happily ever after.